GARGOYLES
DEMONA'S REVENGE

DEMONA'S REVENGE

by Francine Hughes

A PARACHUTE PRESS BOOK

SCHOLASTIC INC.
New York Toronto London Auckland Sydney

A PARACHUTE PRESS BOOK
Parachute Press, Inc.
156 Fifth Avenue
New York, NY 10010

With special thanks to Hunter Heller, Lisa Ramee,
and Robyn Tynan-Winters.

Printed in the U.S.A.
November 1995
ISBN: 0-590-59884-8
A B C D E F G H I J

PROLOGUE

New York City: Present Day

My name is Hudson. I am a Gargoyle, and my home is New York City. But I did not always have a name. And I did not always live here—among towering gray skyscrapers and noisy traffic.

One thousand years ago, hundreds of other Gargoyles and I lived in Castle Wyvern in Scotland. The castle stood alone, built high on a jagged cliff. Ocean waves battered its rocky shore.

Our mission was to protect the castle and all who lived there. We watched over the prince; his daughter, Princess Katharine; and all their people.

By day we slept perched on top of the towers. We were frozen in place like stone statues. We scared away attackers. And by night—we came to life, strong and powerful. We fought anyone who dared to attack the castle. But we had to be careful. We can bleed like humans do when we come alive. And we can die.

We guarded the castle. And we did it well. Still, the humans feared us. Hated us, you might say.

Why?

Because we were different. Because we weren't human.

But there was one human who was our friend. He was the captain of the castle guards. And he liked the Gargoyles much better than he liked humans. He knew that without our help, the castle would have been destroyed long ago.

So the captain made a secret deal with the castle's enemies, the Vikings. The captain would let them attack the castle—destroying all humans. But they were to leave the Gargoyles alone.

The night the Vikings were going to attack, the captain tried to send us away. To have us out of harm's way. He said we should search the countryside for enemies. But Goliath—our leader at the time—took only me. He ordered the others to stay behind and guard the castle.

One Gargoyle thought it was too dangerous to separate. She begged and pleaded with Goliath to change his mind. To stay behind or take the others, too.

Her name was Demona. And she was Goliath's closest friend.

"You are too trusting!" she told Goliath. "Too eager to please humans." But Goliath stood firm.

So we set out at night, Goliath and I. We searched the woods for miles and miles. But we did not see anyone. For the enemy was already at the castle gates. Waiting to attack.

The Vikings had lied. They stormed Castle Wyvern at sunrise, when we were turned to stone and could not fight. And they destroyed *everything*—even the Gargoyles.

Goliath and I returned the next night. But we found only destruction—and a small group of Gargoyles who were not hurt. Four in all. Four Gargoyles out of hundreds.

But we could not cry for our friends. We did not have time. We Gargoyles were all blamed for the terrible attack!

The castle magician, the Magus, cast an evil spell on us. A spell that turned us to stone, day *and* night. A spell that ordered us to sleep—until the castle rose above the clouds.

And so we slept. Six Gargoyles. All that were left, we thought. We did not know that another Gargoyle slept, too. One whom we thought had been destroyed. Demona.

Demona had escaped the attackers. She had asked the Magus to put her under the same spell, too. But Demona—once so honest, so true—turned evil over time.

One thousand years passed. An American businessman, David Xanatos, heard the legend of the sleeping Gargoyles. He flew the castle towers to the top of his skyscraper in New York City. And the spell was broken! Now the castle had risen high above the clouds.

We awakened in a strange, new place. Cars. Computers. Planes. TV. Everything seemed odd. But one thing had stayed the same—humans.

First the captain of the guards tricked us. Then Xanatos tricked us. He brought us to life for a purpose. To help him carry out evil deeds. And when we refused, he tried to destroy us. He failed.

But good came forward to fight evil. And we found a loyal friend during our battle with Xanatos: police detective Elisa Maza.

Elisa helped us move away from Xanatos to a new home, the clock tower in downtown Manhattan. It was a place filled with dark shadows and cool, rough stones. It felt like Castle Wyvern. And we felt at home there. Elisa knew we would. And she knew our true nature would have to be kept a secret.

Goliath and Demona already had names. So Elisa helped the others choose names. We became Hudson, Lexington, Broadway, Brooklyn, and Bronx.

Elisa has shown us our new duty—to defend this city. To guard these human citizens.

You see, all humans aren't evil. There are innocent ones—many innocent ones—who need our help. But that is not all. There is also Demona.

Demona lives out there—somewhere. And she's sworn revenge on all humans—revenge for the way they treated Gargoyles in the past.

Demona is determined to rule. But we are determined to stop her!

CHAPTER 1

New York City: Present Day

Six chimes: six P.M. The sun was setting over the clock tower in New York City. The Gargoyles were turning to flesh.

Hudson stretched. *Crack!* The stone around his body split like an eggshell. Gravel flew from his skin. It littered the ledge. Hudson blinked. No cliffs rose before him. No waves beat against a rugged shore. Instead, he perched on a tall, tall building. Giant skyscrapers glowed in the dusky light. A sea of cars and trucks snaked slowly along the streets below.

Hudson had been dreaming again. Dreaming of the past, when he was leader of the Gargoyles. But it was time to wake up now. Time to face the new night.

Next to Hudson, three Gargoyles—wild-haired Brooklyn, big-bellied Broadway, and the playful-looking Lexington—scampered off their perches. Bronx, the Gargoyle watchdog, trotted after them.

"How about waffles with chocolate fudge for breakfast?" Broadway asked his friends. "Come on!"

The five Gargoyles crept around the clock tower. With its old stone walls, the tower reminded Hudson of Wyvern. Still, it *wasn't* the old castle. The towers of Wyvern sat atop the Xanatos skyscraper.

Hudson gazed across the city at the castle that was so much a part of his own past.

"Are you all right?" a deep, gentle voice asked. Hudson turned to face Goliath, the new Gargoyle leader. Goliath's handsome face looked concerned.

Goliath waited patiently for an answer. He straightened his strong, broad shoulders, and his blue-gray skin melted into the darkness of the shadows.

"I am fine," Hudson finally answered. "Just thinking about old times."

Meanwhile, in another part of the city, Detective Elisa Maza's alarm clock went off. It was seven P.M. Her day was about to begin. Elisa worked the night watch on the New York City police force. She did not mind. The late hours made her friendship with Goliath even stronger.

Elisa stood by the dresser mirror and ran a brush through her long, straight hair. *Maybe it will be a quiet night*, she thought. Then she saw a shadow flash across the mirror.

"Demona!" Elisa cried, spinning around.

The evil Gargoyle perched on the skylight above. Demona's eyes glowed with anger. Her spiky red hair stood on end.

Demona leaped through the skylight and shattered the glass. She landed soft as a cat in the center of Elisa's apartment. Then Demona grabbed her laser weapon and aimed right at Elisa's heart. She fired.

Clutching her chest, Elisa moaned

and then crumpled to the floor.

"You have just been poisoned," Demona said in a pleasant voice. Then she snarled, "In twenty-four hours you will be dead."

Elisa propped herself against the dresser. Her eyes followed Demona as she sprang up through the skylight and glided onto the roof.

"There is a cure," Demona called down to Elisa. "But only I have it. Tell Goliath I will be at the old opera house if he wants it."

Demona grinned and disappeared into the night.

With one strong tug, Elisa pulled the dart from her jacket. Then she reached into an inner pocket and pulled out her badge.

Close call, Elisa thought. The badge had stopped the dart. Elisa wasn't poisoned at all. But she had to tell Goliath!

CHAPTER 2

Elisa rushed to the clock tower. She explained to Goliath, Hudson, and the others what Demona had done.

Goliath paced back and forth. Elisa was their only human friend. He couldn't let anything happen to her. She was too important to the Gargoyles—too important to him.

Elisa touched his arm. "I'm okay," she

said. "You don't have to meet Demona. It's a trap."

Broadway punched a fist in the air. "No!" he shouted excitedly. "We have to stop her from trying this again!"

"Yes! Stop her!" Lexington and Brooklyn echoed just as angrily.

"Goliath must go," Hudson explained to Elisa. He spoke quietly but firmly. "If he does not, Demona will know her plan failed. And she *will* try again."

Goliath sighed. He didn't want to fight Demona. A long time ago, they shared a friendship. And he hated to see anyone harmed—Gargoyle or human. But he had to do something.

"Maybe...maybe I can reach her," Goliath said softly. "Show her she is doing wrong. At least I have to try. For there was a time she would listen to me. Perhaps she will again."

He shook his head and turned to his

old friend. "Hudson, come with me."

Broadway leaped to his feet. "I will go also! I will help you!"

The others jumped up, too, eager to help. But Goliath held up his hand—a sign to quiet down.

"No," he told Broadway. "You stay here with Bronx and guard the tower. Brooklyn, you and Lexington take Elisa home. Stay with her until sunrise. Then she will be safc."

Hudson and Goliath sailed from rooftop to rooftop. Coasting on strong, steady winds...swooping on gusts...never flying, but always gliding in the air. That is how Gargoyles travel.

Lightning flickered in the distance. Hudson thought of the many battles he had fought. He had seen many victories. And many losses. He had faced many enemies. But that was when he was younger, stronger.

"Perhaps you should have brought the others," he told Goliath.

"No," Goliath answered. "They are all too young. I need someone I can rely on. Someone wise. Someone who knows Demona's ways."

The city stretched before them. Lights blinked off one by one as the city went to sleep. Goliath pointed to a rooftop in the distance. "There it is," he said. "The opera house."

A minute later, the Gargoyles dropped onto the roof. Darkness settled over them like a cloak. Hudson squinted. His eyes were not as sharp as they used to be. But he would not give up.

Hudson and Goliath searched among the chimney stacks for signs of Demona. Nothing.

Hudson searched some more—and finally spotted something. Fresh claw marks in the tar!

Hudson motioned Goliath over. “She was here,” he whispered. “And just a few minutes ago.”

They followed the tracks to the foot of a tall, crumbling chimney stack.

A spark of lightning suddenly flooded the roof with light. In a flash, Demona swooped down from the chimney top. She whipped a laser weapon from her belt. In a quick motion, she pointed the laser toward Goliath.

A thunderclap rocked the building. She fired.

“No!” cried Hudson. He hurled himself forward to block the deadly beam. But it was too late. The shot hit Goliath full force in the chest, and he tumbled to the floor.

Hudson raced to Goliath. He drew his sword to shield him from another hit.

Demona grinned and took aim. “You can’t stop me!” she growled. She fired again. Her laser cut through the darkness.

Hudson raised his sword and stepped forward.

ZZZZIP! The laser beam hit the blade. It shot back to Demona like a boomerang.

"Oh!" cried Demona. The beam struck her laser weapon, knocking it away. As she leaped to catch the weapon, she fell from the roof.

Down, down, down she dropped along with the laser. She snatched the weapon. Then she dug her other claws into the building to stop her fall, leaving deep tracks in the old brick.

In the meantime, Hudson quickly dragged the wounded Goliath into the shadows. If only he could hide him. All he needed was a few hours. Then it would be daylight. They would all turn to stone. They would sleep. And while

Goliath slept, his wound would heal.

Sleep was the great healer for all the Gargoyles. Goliath would wake up as strong as ever. Ready for action.

Demona clawed her way up the wall. Then she scrambled back onto the rooftop. She threw back her shoulders and gripped the laser tightly. Her mouth was set in a tight, hard line.

"Well done, old soldier," she called out into the darkness. "But it will end the same for you. No matter what."

"It is not long until sunrise," Hudson warned her from the shadows. "We will all change soon."

"You will never make it to sunrise," Demona sneered.

She leaped high onto a chimney top. Her eyes swept the dark roof. She hunted for her enemies.

Lightning struck. Demona caught sight of Hudson and Goliath in its glow.

They were huddled next to a skylight.

"Now I have you," she muttered.

Her eyes locked with Hudson's. She pressed the trigger.

We have to jump, Hudson thought quickly. He grabbed Goliath and leaped through the skylight. Glass splintered as they crashed down into the opera house and right through the wooden stage.

THUD! They landed hard on the cold basement floor.

Hudson dragged Goliath into a corner.

"Leave me," Goliath whispered.

"Never!" Hudson answered. "The dawn will heal you. We can hold out until then."

The floor creaked above them. Demona! She was inside the opera house.

"Give it up, old one," Demona cried. Her voice echoed through the halls of the huge, empty theater.

A second later, she peered through the hole in the stage.

"You can run," she called. "But you cannot hide." Gracefully she glided down to the basement.

"In fact, you cannot even run." Demona snickered, searching for them in the darkness.

Hudson pulled Goliath deeper into the shadows. He gripped his sword tighter and held it in front of him like a shield.

The storm continued. The loud thunder made Hudson think about a similar storm a long, long time ago. There was nothing to do now but hide and think. Hide till sunrise. And think about the past.

CHAPTER 3

Scotland: One Thousand Years Ago

BOOM! The sound of thunder rumbled through Castle Wyvern. In the royal chambers, eight-year-old Princess Katharine bolted up in bed.

Katharine wasn't frightened by the storm. She'd grown used to the thunder and flashes of lightning—and the sheets of rain lashing against the castle walls.

Princess Katharine wanted to stay up for a special feast that night.

"Father," she said to Prince Malcolm, "I want to see the jugglers!"

The prince gazed into her pretty face. "Hush, now," he said. Then he teased, "The Gargoyles will get you if you don't behave."

A burst of lightning lit the chamber. Eerie shadows danced across the room.

A strange figure stood in one corner. He seemed almost human—with dark skin, a gentle face, and a white beard. But he had sharp, pointy ears. And fangs. He had claws that clicked against the stone floor. And a long tail that thumped behind him.

And strangest of all, he had great wings that rose from his shoulders, then wrapped around him like a cloak.

Katharine gasped.

It was a Gargoyle. The Gargoyle who

would later be called Hudson.

"It is only I, Princess," Hudson said gently. Then he turned to the prince. "Your Highness, we must speak."

The prince led Hudson to the balcony of the princess's chamber. "You should not frighten the girl with stories of Gargoyles," Hudson told him. "We would never harm her."

Prince Malcolm waved his hand in the air. "Oh, do not worry," he said, laughing. "You are much too sensitive." Then his face grew serious. "You are here about the Archmage?"

"Yes," Hudson answered.

The Archmage was an evil wizard. He had tried to take over the prince's throne by magic. But he had failed. And he had been banished from the kingdom.

"I do not think his threats have ended," Hudson told the prince. "Banishment is not enough."

Prince Malcolm scowled. "Let the Archmage dare return. I will—"

"Die!" shouted a voice. Then a flash of lightning swept down from the sky. It blazed long and brightly, with all the colors of the rainbow. Finally it struck a large stone pot next to the prince. THWACK! The pot shattered to bits.

A second lightning bolt struck. And suddenly, the evil magician stood before them. His long, flowing beard gleamed in the moonlight. His black robes swirled in the wind.

In one hand, he held an ancient book of spells called the *Grimorum Arcanorum*. In the other, he held a long, thin wand.

"Archmage!" shouted the prince.

"You thought you could banish me?" the Archmage cried. "Think again, Prince Malcolm!"

The Archmage began to chant,

Demona has an evil plan to get rid of Goliath for good!

Goliath and Hudson hear of Demona's plan and glide off into the night to search for her.

Hudson raises his sword as he and Goliath face Demona in battle!

Goliath is wounded!

"Swear loyalty to me!" Demona cries out to Hudson and Goliath. "Join me and rule the world!"

As Goliath and Hudson escape from Demona, Hudson remembers a time long ago when he was the Gargoyle leader...

...and battled a terrible enemy. It was the Archmage, a wicked wizard, who had an evil plan.

The Archmage poisoned the prince of Castle Wyvern.

Hudson called upon Goliath and Demona to help him search for the Archmage and the cure to the poison.

They discovered the Archmage in a secret cave, and Goliath attacked!

Goliath found the cure to the poison in the Archmage's book of magic spells.

After the battle against the Archmage, Hudson passed his leadership to Goliath.

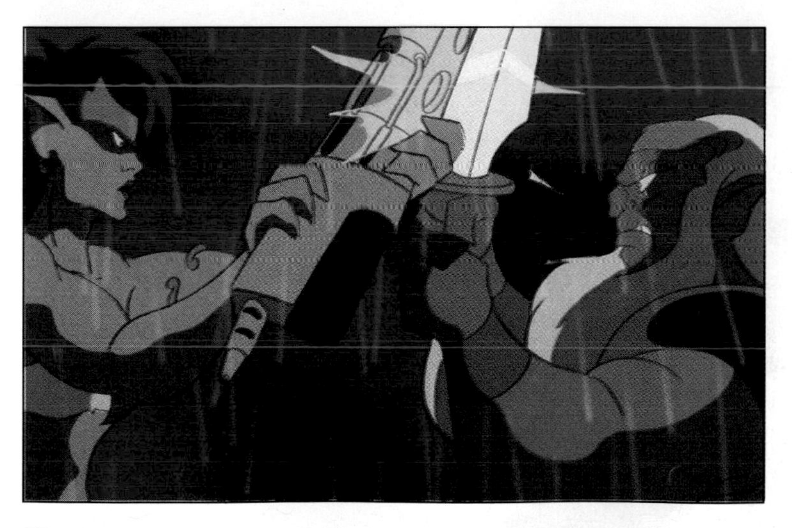

Hudson is suddenly jolted back to the present—and the battle against Demona continues!

As the sun begins to rise, the battle will cease for the night.

After a day's sleep, Goliath and Hudson escape from Demona and soar off to join their friends!

"Fulminus benite. Fulminus benite."

A lightning bolt sliced through the sky like an arrow. And before Hudson could move, the bolt struck him. He fell back against the wall.

"I want revenge," the Archmage bellowed. He lifted the wand to his lips. He blew. And a small deadly dart flew toward Prince Malcolm.

Hudson stumbled to his feet. He had to save the prince! Hudson sprang forward and reached for the dart. His hand stretched forward. Closer. Closer. But he missed!

The dart struck the prince deep in his chest.

"Aha!" The Archmage laughed. Then he disappeared in a burst of light.

With a cry of pain, the prince dropped to the floor. Hudson knelt beside him.

"Get away from him!" Katharine shrieked as she ran out to the balcony.

"Get away! Leave him alone!"

Hudson knew Katharine feared him. *And,* he thought sadly, *I know she will blame me for this.* Quietly he stepped aside.

Katharine threw herself on her father. She sobbed wildly, her tears mixing with the rain. But Hudson did not hear her cries. They were muffled by the loudest roar of thunder yet.

The next night Prince Malcolm lay in bed, feverish and ill. Princess Katharine sat by her father's feet.

Torchlights flickered in the royal chamber. A fire roared in the grate. But Prince Malcolm shivered with cold.

Hudson stood guard as the Magus tended the prince.

"What is it?" Prince Malcolm moaned. "What is wrong with me?"

"You've been poisoned," the Magus

told the prince. "And the poison is strong—made stronger by a magic spell."

"Can you cure me?" the prince asked weakly.

The Magus laid a cool hand on the prince's fevered brow. Then he lowered his eyes. He could not meet his gaze. "Perhaps...if I had the *Grimorum Arcanorum*. The cure is in its pages."

Katharine whirled to face Hudson. "You caused this!" she shouted. Her voice was tight with fury. Her hands clenched in rage. She feared her father would die.

Prince Malcolm waved to his nurse. "Take my daughter away," he said.

As the nurse led the princess from the room, the prince turned to Hudson. "I know it was not your fault," he said. "The princess is young. She does not understand."

Hudson bowed his shoulders. "No. The princess is right. I failed you." Then he slowly walked over to the balcony and climbed up to the castle tower.

For the moment, the storm had passed. A bright moon peeked out from light puffy clouds. But Hudson's spirits stayed dark and heavy.

Below, waves beat against the shore. Hudson knew the storm would return—more fierce than ever.

Slowly Hudson lifted his eyes. There stood Goliath and Demona, wings spread.

"They look so young and strong," Hudson murmured to himself.

"You sent for us?" Goliath asked.

Hudson nodded. "Yes. I will need your help. We must find the Archmage and retrieve the magic book."

"Whatever you command, we will do," Goliath said.

Hudson's face was full of worry. "I cannot fail again. We must hurry. If we do not find the wizard before dawn, all will be lost."

Goliath nodded. "We are with you," he told Hudson.

But Demona stayed silent. Finally she turned to Goliath. "I have never seen him look so old," Hudson heard her whisper to Goliath. "Perhaps it is time he stepped down."

"His age brings wisdom," Goliath whispered back. "That is why he leads."

Hudson dove off the tower. Goliath followed. Demona remained for a moment. Then she shrugged. Lifting her wings, she took off behind them.

CHAPTER 4

New York City: Present Day

Thud, thud. Demona's footsteps brought Hudson back to the present. Back to the opera house. Away from his memories of the days long ago.

"Your game is hopeless, Hudson," Demona called out.

She cast her eyes about the basement. "You were too old to play a thousand years ago. And now Goliath's time is over too. I am the leader now!"

Another flash of lightning pierced the sky. For one long moment, light flooded the basement. Hudson spotted Demona a few feet away. Desperately he pulled Goliath deeper into the shadows.

"Swear loyalty to me!" Demona ordered. "And I will let you live! Join me and rule the world. All you must do is speak!"

Hudson remained silent. They had to find a way outside. They had to escape!

His eyes studied the dust-filled room. There! A window leading up to the street. And a ladder lay nearby. Perfect!

"You say nothing?" Demona's voice rose in anger. "Very well, then. Die!"

She let loose a stream of laser shots. Beams crisscrossed the basement. They covered every inch of space. But Hudson had already pulled Goliath up through the window to safety.

Outside, the street was dark. Empty. *But not for long*, Hudson thought. *Demona will be here. Searching.*

Then Hudson spied a grating in the ground. Another escape route!

Quickly he lifted the cover. Carrying Goliath on his back, the old Gargoyle climbed down.

A moment later, his claws touched ground. He let Goliath slip from his shoulders. Water slapped at their feet. Hudson peered into the blackness. They were in some sort of tunnel. Maybe part of the city water system.

Demona's voice floated into the tunnel. "What?" she shouted. "Are you foolish enough to go underground? Where you cannot use your wings?"

Hudson held Goliath tightly. Carefully he helped him plod through the dark passageway.

As they crept farther through the tunnel, Goliath grew weaker and weaker.

Then he stumbled. "It is hopeless, Hudson," he said. "Go on without me. Save yourself."

Hudson tightened his grip on Goliath's shoulder. "We go together, lad. Or we do not go at all."

"I admire your courage," Demona sneered.

Hudson whipped around. Demona stood behind them. With her laser pointed right at him. "But it is useless," she added.

Hudson peered down. Water swirled at their knees, rushing to the tunnel's end, then disappearing over a ledge. The ledge was only inches away.

Hudson strained forward. The water roared out of the tunnel into a giant waterfall. And the waterfall plunged deep into the Hudson River!

Hudson stepped close to the ledge. They were caught between the waterfall and Demona. Trapped!

Demona raised her laser. Hudson had no choice. He leaped over the edge, clutching Goliath under his left wing. Together they hurtled down the raging waterfall...deep into the river's muddy water.

They burst to the surface, gasping for air. Hudson gathered all his strength. Slowly he towed Goliath to the shore.

At last they reached land. Goliath crawled onto the dirt. He was coughing, struggling to breathe.

Hudson cradled him in his wings. "Stay with me, lad," he pleaded. "We have been in worse scrapes than this. Remember the Archmage's cave..."

CHAPTER 5

Scotland: One Thousand Years Ago

Hudson remembered it all so clearly. Storm clouds were drifting over a full moon in the wild, untamed forest. There before him was the entrance to a cave.

"The Archmage is here!" he told Goliath and Demona. Lighting a torch, he stepped into the cave. "We must get that book!"

Outside, Demona paused. "You're younger. Stronger," she whispered to Goliath. "You should lead. Why should we follow the old one into a cave? Our wings will be useless!"

"We cannot give up now!" Hudson called out. "I will not fail the prince again."

Goliath ducked in after him. "He is our leader," he whispered back to Demona. "And I will not let him do this alone."

Demona stamped one clawed foot in anger. But she followed.

Inside, the cool, damp air pressed against them. They followed a long, twisting tunnel. Strange carvings marked the smooth walls—pictures of snakes and magic potions and horrible battles. Hudson gasped. He'd never seen anything like it.

The tunnel ended in a large open

space—the Archmage's cavern. Giant rocks towered above them like cliffs. Strange jagged rocks hung down from the ceiling. They gleamed like icicles. And right before them, the ground split open in a bottomless pit.

The Archmage! The evil wizard stood on the other side of the pit! All around him fiery torches blazed to light the dark cave.

In his hand the wizard held the *Grimorum Arcanorum*.

"*Fulminus benite*," the Archmage began to chant, pointing a bony hand at the Gargoyles.

A crackling sound filled the air. Thunderbolts flashed from the magician's fingertips and shot across the pit.

Hudson dodged them. But the Archmage was ready to strike again.

"Your time is over, Gargoyles!" the Archmage cried.

"No!" Hudson shouted, leaping onto a big rock. "We have come for the *Grimorum*!"

CRACK! A fiery bolt blasted the rock to pieces. Hudson fell and was buried in a pile of stones.

This is it, he thought sadly. *I have failed.*

Suddenly, Demona shrieked her loudest battle cry. And Goliath vaulted over a rocky ledge. Gliding through the air, he crossed the pit.

Goliath crashed into the Archmage. They both tumbled to the ground.

"No!" cried the Archmage as the ancient book flew from his grasp. It sailed high, then fell deep into the pit.

Goliath scrambled to the edge and dove down. He caught the book in midair. Then he clawed his way up the pit wall. Demona quickly leaped to the side of the pit and helped him out.

The Archmage roared with anger. "Filthy beast! Give me that book!" He grabbed a sharp stone and raced straight for Goliath.

"Goliath!" Demona cried out in warning.

Demona and Goliath threw themselves to the ground. And the Archmage tumbled past them—down into the bottomless pit.

"Ahhh!" He screamed until his evil voice faded away.

CHAPTER 6

New York City: Present Day

The mighty Gargoyles had defeated the Archmage on that day long ago. But now the stakes were different—maybe even higher. Now there was another battle. Against one of their own. Against an evil Gargoyle—Demona!

Time pressed on. It was almost dawn. Hudson and Goliath were almost safe.

All they needed was a place to hide.

Hudson helped Goliath through the trees. Finally they came to a cemetery. Tall headstones rose from the ground. Mausoleums—old stone buildings filled with tombs—dotted the graveyard.

The wind began to howl. Raindrops splattered the ground. Hudson had to keep Goliath safe and warm until sunrise. But where? Inside a mausoleum—that was it!

With all his strength, Hudson pushed open a mausoleum door. Quickly Hudson dragged Goliath inside.

"Stay here, lad," he said. "I will be back for you."

Goliath tried to stand. "You cannot face Demona alone," he whispered.

"I can face her," Hudson answered. *I just cannot beat her*, he added to himself.

Hudson stepped outside. Rain pelted

his face. He crouched, then dashed to a nearby tree for cover.

"Join me and rule the world!" Hudson heard Demona's voice carry over the wind. But where was she?

Hudson whirled around. There she stood, in front of the mausoleum. Would she see Goliath huddled inside? Hudson had to attack. Now!

He drew his sword and rushed toward Demona.

Demona swung her laser like a club and blocked the blow. "Now you will suffer!" she cried, leaping onto the mausoleum roof.

Hudson sprang up after her. They slipped and slid on the wet roof. Their weapons met again and again. Lightning flashed and thunder boomed.

Bit by bit, Demona wore Hudson down.

"This is the end!" she shouted. She

grasped her weapon, ready to strike one final time.

"No!" Goliath roared below. Shutting his eyes in pain, he lifted himself onto the roof. His legs trembled as he straightened. He reached out to grab Demona's laser.

Demona froze, surprised. Then she grinned with evil joy. "So good of you to join us!" she said, yanking the weapon free from Goliath's grip.

Hudson lunged between them. He raised his sword high. But Demona knocked it away.

"I am smarter," she snarled. "Stronger. And younger!"

Hudson drew in a deep breath. Then he spread his wings to shield his friend. "That may be true. But I know something you do not. Something that comes only with age."

In an instant the sun began to rise,

blazing through the clouds.

"I know how to wait," Hudson added.

It was dawn.

"Nooooo!" cried Demona.

But it was too late. She couldn't attack. She couldn't even move. The Gargoyles had turned to stone.

CHAPTER 7

Scotland: One Thousand Years Ago

Hudson dreamed of Scotland...of returning to the castle with the ancient book of magic spells.

Inside Prince Malcolm's chambers, nurses hurried about. They smiled and laughed as they worked, for everything was going to be fine.

"The cure is complete," the Magus

told Hudson. "The prince will recover."

Prince Malcolm sighed. Then he reached for Hudson's hand.

"Thank the stars you were able to bring the *Grimorum* in time," he whispered faintly.

Hudson hung his head in shame. "I did not save you," he admitted. "You should thank another."

Hudson could not take credit for the deed. He knew it was Goliath who had fought the Archmage so bravely. If it weren't for Goliath, they may not have won the *Grimorum Arcanorum*—and saved the prince.

Hudson felt tired and longed for rest. His bones were weary. So he returned to the castle tower.

For a moment Hudson listened to the young Gargoyles talk.

"The clan needs a new leader," Demona said.

Goliath shook his head. "You are absolutely wrong, Demona."

"No, she is right," Hudson interrupted. "It is time for me to step down." He gazed into Goliath's eyes. "And for you to lead."

Goliath stepped back. "No!" he cried. "You led us to the Archmage! It was your skill! Not mine. I cannot take command now."

Hudson placed a hand on young Goliath's shoulder. "It is time, my friend."

Goliath fell silent. He gazed deep into Hudson's eyes, and reluctantly he nodded. "Then I shall. But you must stay by my side. I will need your wisdom."

The two warriors—one old, one young—clasped hands.

CHAPTER 8

New York City: Present Day

The sun set over the Hudson River. At the cemetery, three stone statues cracked. Bits of rock flew through the air. And the Gargoyles turned to flesh.

"Now it ends!" Demona cried, lifting the laser above her head.

Hudson grabbed the weapon and twisted it away. Behind him Goliath rose. His wings stretched wide. Sleep had helped him. His wound had healed. Once again he was powerful.

Demona backed away. "You think you have won," she cackled. "But you have forgotten why you came. Your human friend is dead by now. The poison has run its course."

Then she soared off in a gust of wind.

Goliath grinned at Hudson. "Elisa is alive, of course. But let us keep that a secret for now."

Just as they had in the past, the two clasped hands. "Thank you for keeping me alive," Goliath said. "There is no one else I would rather have at my side."

Hudson chuckled. "And I thought my warrior days were over."

But really, he decided, the present was not so very different from the past. There were poisons. Battles. Tests of loyalty.

And just as before, Hudson would do his duty. He would guard and protect—but with Goliath as his leader.

The two old friends soared into the night.